Cover art and illustrations by Shaun Moffett.

Published June 2018

Crowned Stag
701 Bullock Place
Lexington, KY 40508
www.crownedstag.com

Thor was a dinosaur through and through. He had a long tail and a long neck too.

All through the forest he would stomp, stomp, stomp.
Looking for a tasty tree to chomp, chomp, chomp.

But every time he'd find
a yummy treat over there
his friends would beat him to it
and just strip the tree bare.

"Thor the Pokey Dinosaur!"
they'd laugh and they'd shout,
but Thor was not the kind of guy
to sit down and pout.

Off to the garage he went
with ratchet in hand.
Off to be the fastest dinosaur
in the land!

He found an old clunker, and he chopped off the top.
The nuts and bolts were flying all around his small shop.

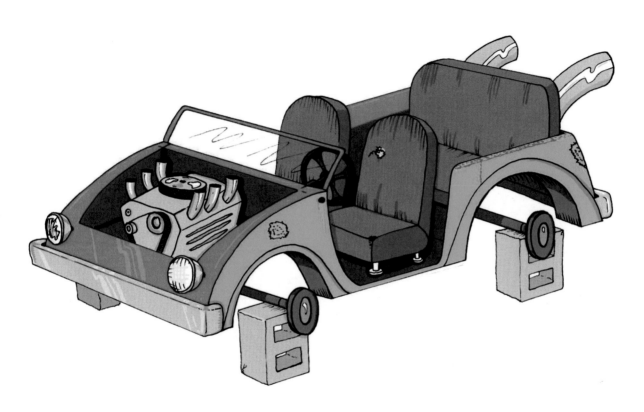

**Souped up the engine. Put on dual exhausts.
Any part that made the car feel heavy got tossed.**

Day after day and night after night
Thor worked on his car 'til everything looked right.

One final touch so that it wouldn't look tame. All across the front he painted...

orange

and

yellow

flames!

Thor jumped in the driver's seat and twisted the key...

**The engine thundered loud
and Thor giggled with glee!**

He saw his friends heading for a nice leafy tree.
Time to see how fast his hot rod turned out to be.

He pressed the gas pedal. Tires spun and smoked.

"We'll see who's pokey now!" Thor laughed and joked.

The car shot forward.
Thor's head leaned back.
He gripped the steering wheel
and zoomed toward his snack.

Thor's friends heard a sound louder than they could roar. They had never seen a thing moving that fast before!

Thor yelled, "Excuse me!"
as he whizzed on by.
His friends just stood there
blinking their eyes.

Thor hit the brakes and slid his car to a stop.
Right next to the tree with tasty leaves on the top.

He jumped out of his car and began his leaf feast.
His friends caught up as he chewed his last piece.

"Nice wheels!"

"So fast!"

"I'm digging the flames!"

Thor loved his hot rod and his friends felt the same.

Thor said, "Calling me pokey made me feel bad inside...

but I forgive you.

Hop in and let's all take a ride!"

Thor's friends said, "We're sorry... thanks for staying our friend!"
They all piled in the car and sped off...

THE END

37727281R00019

Made in the USA
Lexington, KY
30 April 2019